For Mom and Dad

First U.S. edition 1993
Published in Great Britain in 1993 by Walker Books Ltd., London.

Library of Congress Cataloging-in-Publication Data

Vulliamy, Clara.
Ellen and Penguin / Clara Vulliamy.
Summary: A young girl and her stuffed penguin are too shy to
join in the fun at the playground, until they make friends
with another bashful girl and her toy monkey.
ISBN 1-56402-193-9
[1. Bashfulness—Fiction.   2. Friendship—Fiction.   3. Toys—Fiction.
4. Play—Fiction.]   I. Title.
PZ7.V994E1   1993
[E]—dc20   92-54590

10 9 8 7 6 5 4 3 2 1

Printed in Italy

The pictures in this book were done in watercolors.

Candlewick Press
2067 Massachusetts Avenue
Cambridge, Massachusetts 02140

ELLEN
AND
PENGUIN

CLARA VULLIAMY

CANDLEWICK PRESS
CAMBRIDGE, MASSACHUSETTS

Ellen was still very small.

Penguin was even smaller.

Ellen could
dress herself

and put on
her own shoes.

But Penguin had to be helped.

He made a silly fuss and kept waving

his flippers around.

When it was time to go to the park,
Penguin felt safer in Ellen's coat pocket.

He got a little scared out in the street

and snuggled down even deeper.

In the park there was a big playground.

Ellen and Penguin watched the older children

playing on high walkways

and whizzing down the slide. Penguin
wouldn't go on anything. He said it made him
feel sick just to look.

So Ellen took him to feed

the sparrows and blackbirds.

But when the big geese

chased the little birds away,

Penguin decided

it was time to go.

By the garden, some dolls and teddies

were having a tea party,

but Penguin was too shy to join in.

Ellen tried playing catch with the other children, but Penguin wasn't much help.

And he was a terrible goalie.

"We don't want to play with you anymore," the others said.

"You're no good."

Penguin felt really horrible.

He wanted to go home.

Then, over in a corner,
Ellen saw another little girl
standing on her own.
She was holding a
scruffy gray monkey.

"Come on, Penguin,"
said Ellen. "Be brave."

She took a deep breath. "This is Penguin."
"This is Bill," said the girl, "and I'm Jo.
I want to go on the slide, but Bill is
too frightened to be left on his own."

Ellen and Jo sat Penguin and Bill down
together so they wouldn't get lonely. Then
they had a great time taking turns on the slide.

Penguin tried too, but he wanted

Ellen to hold on to his flipper very tightly.

Bill preferred to watch.

Penguin said they'd probably be awake all
night being excited about tomorrow.

But while he talked and talked,

Ellen fell fast asleep.